# The Barefoot Book of
# Knights

*For Emrys, some more stories — J. M.*
*A Franco e Berlin amici preziosi — G. M.*

Barefoot Books
2067 Massachusetts Ave
Cambridge, MA 02140

This book has been printed on 100% acid-free paper
The illustrations were prepared in china ink and watercolor on 100% cotton 300gsm watercolor paper
Design by Jennie Hoare, Bradford on Avon
Typeset in 11.5 Semper roman
Color separation by Grafiscan, Verona
Printed and bound in China by PrintPlus Ltd.

Hardcover ISBN 1-84686-034-2

The Library of Congress cataloged the first hardcover edition as follows:

Matthews, John, 1948-
  The Barefoot book of knights / written by John Matthews ; illustrated by Giovanni Manna.
    p. cm.
  Contents: The Knight of the Kitchen (Britain) -- The Knight of the Swan (Germany) -- The three journeys
of Ilya Murom (Russia) -- Perronik the fool (Brittany) -- The tale of Gushtasp (Persia) -- Yogodayu and the
army of bees (Japan) -- Sir Cliges and the cherry tree (France) -- The world of knights and chivalry.
  Summary: A kindly armorer weaves tales of true chivalry from around the world so that a young page
might learn and reach his ultimate goal of knighthood.
  ISBN 1-84148-205-6
1. Knights and knighthood--Folklore. [1. Knights and knighthood--Folklore.] I. Manna, Giovanni, 1966- ill. II.
Title.

PZ8.1.M433Bar 2005
398.22--dc22

                              2004021456

                        3 5 7 9 8 6 4 2

*The Barefoot Book of*

# Knights

*written by* John Matthews

*illustrated by* Giovanni Manna

Barefoot Books
*Celebrating Art and Story*

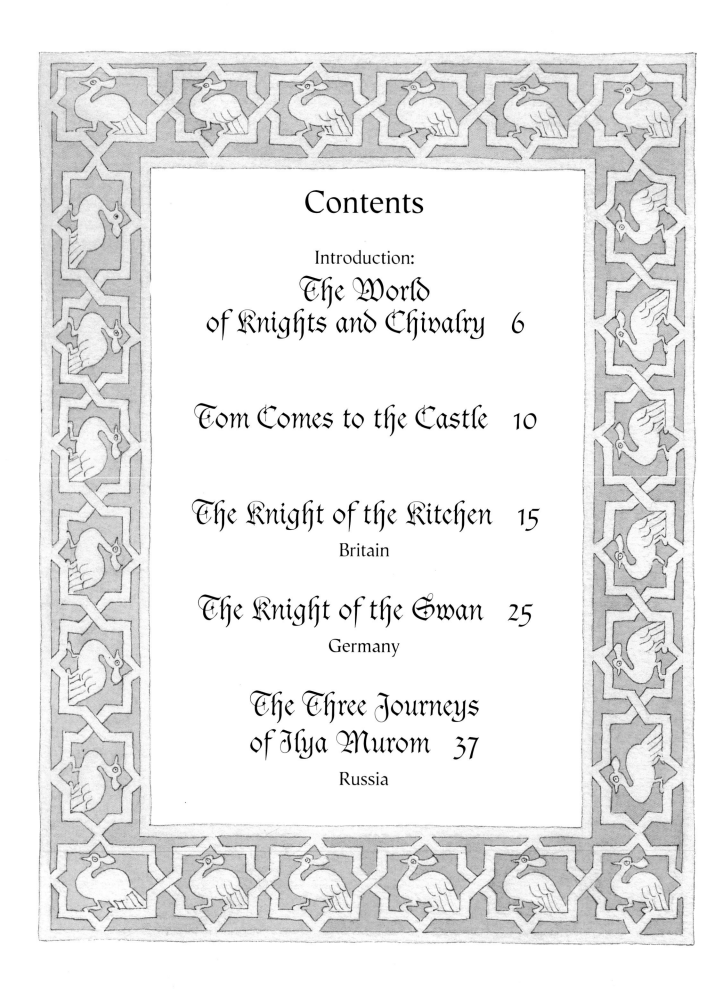

# Contents

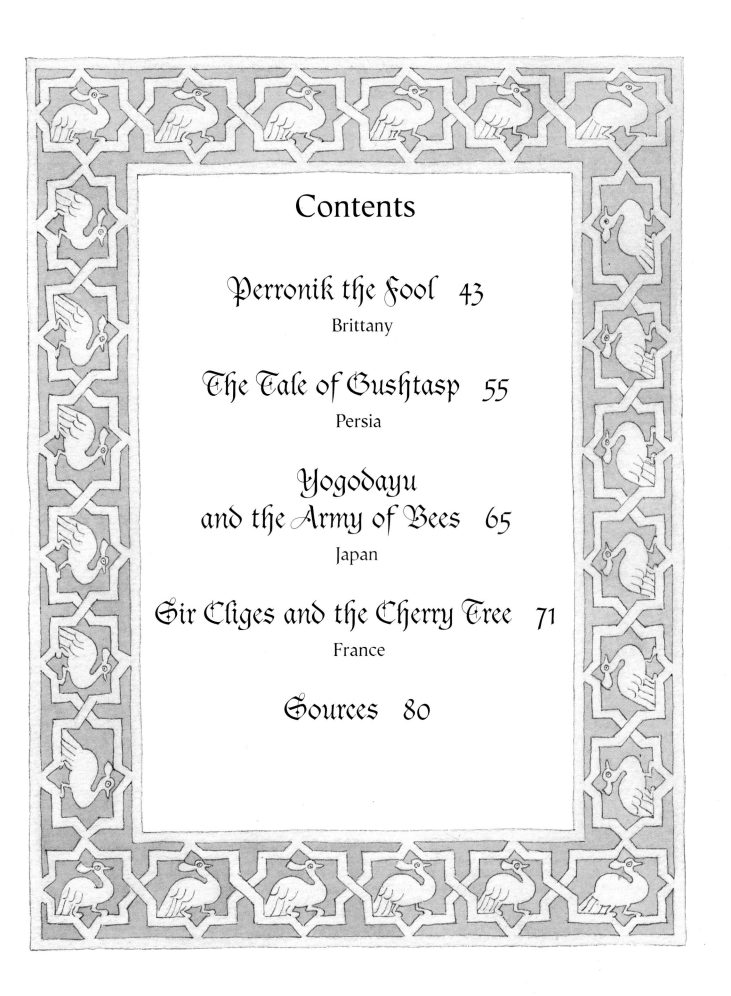

# Contents

# The World of Knights and Chivalry

The idea of knighthood goes back to the time of Ancient Rome, when the emperor's personal bodyguards were known as "miles" or knights. But the most familiar picture of the knight comes from the Middle Ages, which lasted from about the tenth to the fifteenth century A.D. This is when we first see these mounted warriors, clad in armor and bearing a sword, shield and spear, riding into battle at the side of kings like Arthur or Richard the Lionheart.

In fact, the concepts of knighthood and chivalry (the code by which knights behaved) had evolved over a long period of time. People knew them from as early as the ninth century A.D., though it was not for another hundred years or so that they began to tell stories of famous individual knights, like the ones in this book. In Europe, knighthood evolved at the same time as the feudal system. Under this system, knights gave their fealty (a promise to serve) to a great nobleman who, in return, provided the knights with a horse, weapons and a place to live. This gave the nobles their own private armies and, since they owed fealty to the king, when the king went to war, the nobles and their knights went along with him.

Like Tom, boys from the age of nine or ten were apprenticed to a knight to be trained in the arts of correct behavior, good manners and skill with horse and weapons. This training usually lasted between six and eight years and fell into three stages. When they first arrived at the home of the knight, they became pages, with duties ranging from work in the kitchens to caring for the horses. Then, around age twelve or thirteen, they became squires, progressing to a more formal level of training. They virtually became personal servants to the lord, waiting on him and keeping his armor and weapons cleaned and polished. Squires wore silver spurs as a sign of their status. Finally, when they reached sixteen or seventeen, they became knights themselves, if their families could afford it.

6

This generally involved quite an elaborate ceremony. First, the squire took a special ceremonial bath, to show that he was washing away any old, bad habits and preparing himself for his new life. Then, he usually spent the night alone in a church or chapel, with his sword laid before him on the altar, thinking about the duties he would undertake as a knight. This was known as a vigil.

In the morning, the candidate proceeded either to the main hall of the castle or to the courtyard. There, in the presence of all the other pages and squires as well as most of the household, he was formally made a knight. The lord himself struck the knight lightly on the shoulder (this was called the buffet or the dubbing) and helped to fasten on a new set of gold or gilded spurs in token of his new rank.

After this, depending on how wealthy his family was, the new knight either continued to serve the lord in whose house he had been trained, or returned to his own lands and himself became a lord with pages, squires and knights in his service.

During their time as pages and squires, the would-be knights learned about the code of chivalry by which all knights were expected to live. This was based on the idea of the strong caring for the weak. All knights were required to help people in distress, especially women and children, and to behave in an honorable way. They also had to champion right over wrong, uphold the laws of God and the Church, and serve their king with total obedience.

Many of the ideas of chivalry came about when the Church, concerned about general lawlessness and violence, tried to impose order on the warlike lords and their knights by making them take oaths to uphold the peace. This introduced a spiritual dimension into chivalry, which has remained a part of it ever since. It also gave rise to several orders of chivalry, such as the Knights Templar or the Order of St. John of Jerusalem, who were devoted to protecting pilgrims bound for the Holy Land.

Girls did not become knights, since women did not bear arms, but a singular exception was Joan of Arc, a French peasant girl who was inspired by dreams to lead the army of France to victory against the English in 1429. She wore men's clothing and later put on armor — something that would have shocked everyone at that time.

The armor and weapons worn by knights evolved as time went on. In the earliest times, soldiers wore leather armor, on which were sewn metal plates to protect them. At the beginning of the Middle Ages, this was replaced by suits of chain mail, made from woven links of steel. Armor became increasingly elaborate with the passage of time, and, by the fifteenth century, knights went into battle wearing complete suits of steel. These suits weighed so much, the knights often had to be lifted by a kind of crane onto the backs of their horses.

Much of a knight's time was spent in practicing wielding his heavy sword and learning to move quickly in armor, which became increasingly weighty. When they were not directly involved in warfare, the knights arranged tournaments in which they fought each other, both for sport and battle practice.

Sometimes, they engaged in contests where they fought each other on a field divided in two by a wooden barrier, called "the lists." The knights would charge toward each other on horseback with their lances lowered and try to knock each other out of the saddle. As well as these single combats, there was a kind of free-for-all fight called a mêlée, in which the knights were divided up into teams and fought each other to a standstill. Prizes were awarded to the best fighters, generally those who were left standing at the end.

As the stories told about knights show us, the reality was often brutal. Despite this, the idea of chivalry never quite died out and, to this day, those who behave with kindness and courtesy toward others are called chivalrous. The figure of the knight himself remains a kind of heroic model on which warriors of many ages have based their own lives.

*John Matthews*

# Tom Comes to the Castle

The castle looked very big and dark when Tom of Warwick first saw it. Like most ten-year-old boys of noble birth, he had been sent away from home to learn about knighthood and chivalry, by first becoming a page and later a squire in the household of a knight. But, after the familiar, comfortable surroundings of his family's manor house, the castle seemed cold and unfriendly.

As a page, Tom knew that he would be asked to do all kinds of tasks, from cleaning the armor of Sir Brian des Isles, whose castle it was, to mucking out the stables and washing up pots and pans in the kitchen. He would also learn how to fight, first of all with sword and dagger and, later, when he was big enough to carry it, with the lance. And he would be taught about chivalry, the code by which all knights lived.

But such things were far from Tom's mind that day. All he could think about were his mother and father and his elder brother, Robert, who was already a squire and might soon become a knight. That was the way of it: at age nine or ten, you became a page; then, at around twelve, you became a squire. If you were lucky, then you got to serve a real knight, looking after his horse and armor and making sure his sword was always sharp. Eventually, if all went well and your family could afford it, you became a knight yourself.

But that was a long way off — maybe another seven years — an age away to Tom. Now, all he could think of was what a big and lonely place the castle looked and how he would have no friends. Even Peter, the servant who had brought him to the castle, would be leaving right away.

Mournfully, Tom followed Peter across the courtyard of the castle toward the entrance to the keep, the huge central building, which was at least five floors high and probably had a dungeon underneath it.

Just before they got to the keep, there was a smaller building, built mostly of timber, which leaned in the shade of the castle's huge walls. Peter led the way in and stood, hesitating, in the doorway. Tom peered around him and saw a long, low room hung with all kinds of weapons and shields and bits of armor. There was straw on the floor and a cheerful fire burning in the fireplace. Several boys, some of his own age, others of maybe fifteen or sixteen, were gathered around, listening to a tall, imposing man with a weather-beaten face. Tom noticed, at once, that he had very large hands and, when he came toward them, he walked with a slight limp.

"You must be young Tom of Warwick," said the man. "I am Master William, the Armorer. It's my job to look after the pages and squires and try to knock a bit of sense into your heads." Although his words were fierce, he smiled at the same time and Tom decided he liked him.

Master William waved his large hands, indicating the whole room. "This will be your home for the next year or so," he said. "You'll sleep here, eat here and learn everything I can teach you about chivalry and knighthood. If you listen well and do as you're told, we shall get along just fine. Any questions?"

Tom shook his head.

"All right, then," said Master William, "there's hot food in the kitchens and, later on, you can get some fresh straw for bedding. Hubert here will go with you."

A boy who looked no older than Tom came forward. They exchanged looks and then Hubert grinned. "Come on, then," he said and led the way outside again toward the great, high keep. As they went, Tom said, "Is Master William a kind teacher?"

"Oh, yes," answered Hubert. "And he knows a million stories. If you're lucky, he'll tell some of them. We always try to persuade him — especially when he wants to tell us about chivalry."

Chatting happily, the two boys entered the castle keep and headed for the kitchens. A rich smell of roasting meat drifted toward them and, for the first time that day, Tom felt better. Maybe it wouldn't be so bad here, after all. And he loved stories more than anything, especially ones about knights and enchantment and fighting dragons. Maybe Master William knew some of those?

One day, it was Tom's turn to work in the kitchen. Usually, he loved the big stone-flagged room in the castle keep, for it always seemed warm and full of bustling people. But, today, he had to help prepare the food for Sir Brian's table, and that meant washing dozens of vegetables and cleaning mountains of greasy pots.

Tom hated it. "How can I learn to be a knight if I have to wash dishes?" he muttered. Master William, who happened to be passing at that moment, heard him. "There are many good reasons," he said. "It's important for you to understand that being a knight doesn't just mean having adventures or rescuing people. It means helping in all kinds of different ways, as well."

"But, surely, knights don't have to work in the kitchen," said Tom, rebelliously.

"As a matter of fact," answered Master William, "one of the best knights in the world started out working as a scullery boy."

Tom's eyes opened wide. "Really?"

"Really," said Master William. "Would you like to hear about him?"

Tom nodded excitedly and followed the Armorer into the stable, where they both sat down on some bales of hay. With a faraway look in his eyes, Master William began...

# The Knight of the Kitchen

A Story from Britain

King Arthur had a rule that he would never sit down to a feast until he had seen or heard of some wondrous thing. Nor did he ever go hungry because, in those days, there were enough wonders to fill every day of the year.

One day then, as the king was waiting to begin a feast, Sir Kay looked out of the window and said, "We can all go in and eat, my lord, for I see a tall young man coming who leans on the shoulders of two others. I am sure this will be a marvel."

So King Arthur and his knights, and Queen Guinevere and her ladies, went into the great hall and waited for the strange youth to appear. He soon entered and he was, indeed, as tall and handsome as Sir Kay had said, though he still leaned on the shoulders of two other men, as if he had not the strength to stand unaided. Right up to the royal dais they went, and there the tall stranger straightened his back and saluted the king.

"Who are you and what is your business here?" asked King Arthur.

"Sire, I would rather not reveal my name until another time," answered the youth. "As to my business, it is only to ask of you that I be fed and housed for one year, from this day."

"That is easily granted," replied the king. "But, surely, there is something else that you would wish for."

"In one year's time, if I may, I will ask a further boon," said the youth. "For now, there is nothing more that I wish for."

"Very well," said King Arthur and he gave the youth into the care of Sir Kay, the Seneschal, whose chief task was to see to the ordering of the food served to the king and his knights. He thought the youth had acted in a manner unbecoming to one who was clearly of noble birth by only asking for food and lodging, and so he decided to make his life as unpleasant as possible.

"Since all you want is bed and board," said Sir Kay, "you can work in the kitchens for a year. And, since you won't give your name, I shall give you one myself." He looked the youth up and down and noticed that he had large white hands. "I shall call you Fairhands," sneered Sir Kay.

So Fairhands went to work in King Arthur's kitchens. For a year, he seldom had anything other than harsh words from Sir Kay. But not once, during all this time, did the youth ever speak up or answer back. Indeed, he became something of a favorite among the rest of the kitchen staff, which only made Sir Kay angrier.

But the year soon passed and it was feast time again. As usual, King Arthur waited for some marvel or adventure to happen. This time, it came in the shape of a damsel asking for a knight to help her mistress, Dame Lioness, who was being held captive against her will by the fearsome Red Knight of the Red Lands. Before King Arthur had time to call forth one of his knights to undertake this task, Fairhands came forward and begged to be given the adventure. "For," he said, "you promised to grant me a boon one year ago and this is my request."

"Very well," said King Arthur, "it shall be as you wish."

But the damsel threw up her hands in horror when she saw Fairhands, still dressed in his greasy scullery clothes. "A kitchen knave!" she cried. "Never will I accept help from such a one!" and, so saying, she rushed from the hall.

"You had best go after her," said King Arthur, as Fairhands hesitated. "The adventure is yours, if you will take it."

So the youth hurried from the hall and outside he met Sir Lancelot, the greatest of King Arthur's knights. "You will need armor and weapons if you are to face the Red Knight," he said. Then he called to his squire to fetch some of his own armor, which he gave to Fairhands.

"Now, you will need a horse," said Sir Lancelot, and called for his second best charger to be saddled.

Stammering out his thanks, Fairhands mounted and rode, as swiftly as he could, after the damsel. He caught up with her at the edge of the forest.

"Get away from me!" cried the lady, angrily. "I can smell you from here."

"I am sorry, my lady," answered Fairhands, "but King Arthur has given me this adventure and pursue it I must."

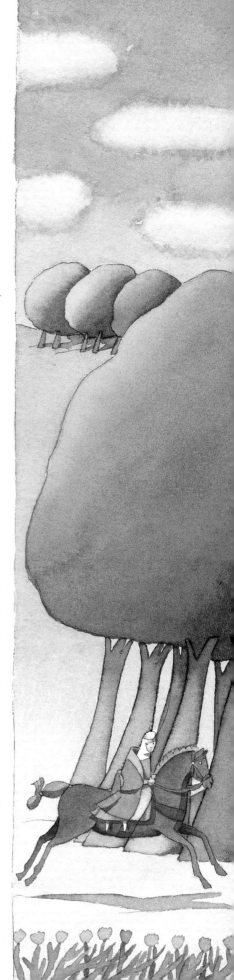

"I suppose I cannot stop you from following me," said the damsel, "but be sure to keep as far away as possible."

"If that is your wish," answered Fairhands, "but may I at least know your name?"

"Linnet," said the damsel, brusquely, and rode on without speaking again.

Soon, they reached a clearing in the forest and there was an old, dark hawthorn tree, with a black shield hanging upon it. In the shade of the tree, on a black horse, sat a knight clad in black armor. When he saw Fairhands and the damsel approaching, he drew his sword. "None may pass this way unless they fight me," he cried harshly.

So Fairhands drew his own sword and the two began to fight. Mighty indeed was that battle but, in the end, Fairhands defeated the Black Knight and sent him to King Arthur to be judged for his crimes, for he had slain many knights who rode that way before. But all the Lady Linnet could say about Fairhands' victory was, "How shameful that a true knight, however bad, should be defeated by a mere scullery boy."

So they rode on in silence and soon came to a clearing, where they met a knight clad in blue armor. Once again, Fairhands was challenged and, once again, he fought mightily, defeating his opponent and sending him to King Arthur. But still the Lady Linnet had nothing good to say to her champion, only commenting on the smell of grease that came from him.

It was the same when Fairhands met and defeated a third knight, who dressed all in green and who was the strongest of the three. But, this time, the damsel remained silent and, if the truth be known, she looked at Fairhands almost with respect after this victory.

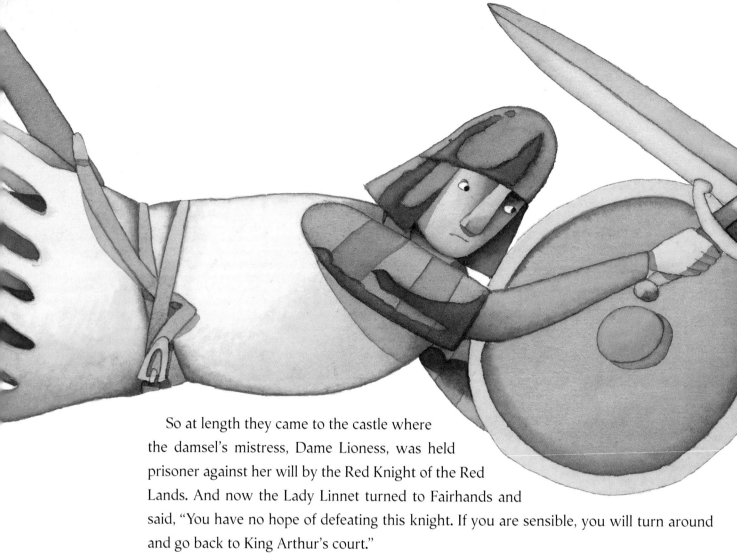

So at length they came to the castle where
the damsel's mistress, Dame Lioness, was held
prisoner against her will by the Red Knight of the Red
Lands. And now the Lady Linnet turned to Fairhands and
said, "You have no hope of defeating this knight. If you are sensible, you will turn around
and go back to King Arthur's court."

Fairhands shook his head. "This is my task, lady. I shall accomplish it or die in the
attempt."

At that moment, the Red Knight himself came thundering up. His armor gleamed like
freshly spilled blood and he rode a red horse that was almost as fierce as himself.

"Who dares to challenge me?" he thundered.

"I come at the bidding of King Arthur," answered Fairhands. "He bids you set Dame
Lioness free."

"Ha!" shouted the Red Knight. "And who is going to make me?"

"I shall try my best," answered Fairhands.

"And who might you be?" demanded the Red Knight.

Fairhands took a deep breath. "My name is Gareth, and I am the youngest son of
King Lot of Orkney," he said.

The Lady Linnet stared at him in astonishment, but the Red Knight merely snorted and drew his sword. "Say goodbye to your lady," he roared and the two began to fight.

If the Black, Blue and Green Knights had been strong opponents, the Red Knight was even stronger. When they began to fight, it was early morning, and they continued all that day until night fell and they were forced to stop and rest. Next day, they began again and, again, they fought until the light was fading. Both were bleeding and exhausted by this time but, in the end, it was Fairhands who struck the final blow, felling the Red Knight to the ground.

"Sir," begged the fallen man, "spare my life, I beg you."

"I will," answered Fairhands, turning to the Lady Linnet, "if this lady will ask it of me."

"Spare him, indeed," answered the damsel. Then she looked at Fairhands. "Sir," she said, "I must beg your forgiveness for the way I have treated you. The truth is that I never saw a braver or a more honorable man."

A smile spread over Fairhands' face, as he helped the battered Red Knight to stand. "You must go to King Arthur and beg his forgiveness," he said.

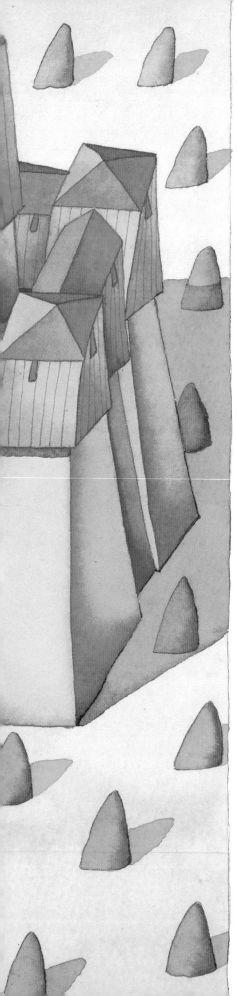

Now, it happened that Dame Lioness had been watching the great battle between Fairhands and the Red Knight from a window in the castle and, as she watched, so she began to fall in love with the youth. Then she rode forth with her attendants and announced that she would personally accompany Fairhands back to King Arthur's court. "For so may I best tell of your great deeds, Sir Knight," she said, and smiled radiantly until the youth blushed and looked away.

So it was that Fairhands, the Lady Linnet and Dame Lioness set out on the road to Camelot, where King Arthur's court was to be found. Many things they spoke of as they traveled and Fairhands explained that he had concealed his true identity, so that he might not receive special favor at court. Soon they reached Camelot and there the king heard about Fairhands' deeds.

There was great rejoicing when it was learned that Fairhands, the kitchen boy, was really Sir Gareth of Orkney. Sir Kay had the grace to look ashamed at the treatment he had meted out to the youth. The king, seeing how Dame Lioness looked upon her champion and how she sighed, would have given his consent to their wedding.

But Fairhands had eyes for no one save the Lady Linnet, with whom he had secretly fallen in love as they traveled together. And when she, too, revealed her true feelings for the "Knight of the Kitchen," they were soon married and lived a long and happy life together. In time, Sir Gareth of Orkney became one of King Arthur's greatest knights and few remembered that he had once worked as a scullery lad in the royal kitchens.

"So you see," Master William said, "even the best knights sometimes have to do things they don't want to do. But, in the end, it all came out right." He stood up. "Now then, off you go to the kitchens and don't forget to clean the pots really well." And Tom hurried off, thinking as he went that, if he carried out his duties really well, maybe he would be sent on a great adventure.

22

23

On a sunny day in summer, the pages and squires were gathered around Master William in the courtyard of the castle to learn about the way knights behaved.

"Chivalry," began Master William, "is the code of behavior by which all knights try to live. It's not enough to be brave and clever or to ride a horse well and swing a sword skillfully. You also have to be kind and generous. Chivalry means behaving as well as you can all the time. And, it means remembering to treat everyone you meet honorably. Not just the lords and ladies, but the poorer people as well. In fact, anyone who asks for help."

"But, how do we know if they're good people?" asked Tom.

"Your heart will nearly always tell you," answered Master William, "and, if it doesn't, your common sense will."

He looked thoughtful. "I believe I know a story about a boy who suffered greatly at the hands of a noble lady who should have been honorable but, in fact, was very bad indeed."

"Tell us!" shouted the pages and squires.

"Well," said Master William, "I suppose you could learn something about chivalry from it..."

# The Knight of the Swan

## A Story from Germany

26

Long ago, in the kingdom of Germany, there lived a king called Orian. One day, when he was out hunting, he became lost. Wandering through unfamiliar lands, he encountered a beautiful lady and her maidens. Although he knew nothing of her birth or parentage, the king fell head over heels in love with her, and, after that, nothing would do but that he must marry her. And so it was done.

Now, this made the king's mother, Queen Matabrunne, very angry indeed, for she had always intended that her son should make a far greater marriage than with this unknown lady. So she vowed to do anything she could to harm his new bride.

Fate decreed that she should soon find a way, for, not long after this, the king went away to war and it happened that, while he was absent, the time came for the young queen to be delivered of their first child. Matabrunne insisted that she should attend her daughter-in-law. Thus it was that she alone was present at the birth, not of one child, but of seven: six boys and one girl. And the greatest wonder of all was that each and every child was born with a chain of silver about its neck.

When she saw this, Matabrunne hated them even more than she hated their mother, for she knew by this sign that they were no ordinary children and that their mother was no ordinary lady. Calling her most faithful and devoted squire, Matabrunne ordered him to take the children to the river and drown them all. Then she made it known throughout the land that the young queen herself had murdered her babies.

When King Orian returned from the war, he found the castle silent and grim. With tears in her eyes, Matabrunne told him what the young queen had done. "We had to lock her in her room until you returned, my son. There is only one punishment for such a crime: death."

The king was horrified by this news. But he could not find it in his heart to kill his wife. Instead, he ordered that she be taken away and shut up in the deepest dungeon of the castle, so that he would never have to see her again.

Meanwhile, the squire who had been ordered to kill the royal infants took them into the forest. But when he looked upon them, he could not bring himself to do as he had been ordered. Instead, he wrapped them in a blanket and left them lying together in a sheltered clearing. Then he returned home and told his mistress that they were dead.

Now, in the forest, there lived a wise hermit and it happened that, as he was walking among the trees, he heard the crying of a baby. Following the sound, he found not one but seven babies, each with a chain of silver links around its neck. Amazed at the sight, the hermit gathered them up in his arms and took them home to the little hut where he lived.

"How shall I care for you?" he wondered, looking around at the poorly furnished dwelling, with cracks in the walls and the roof, and a fire that always seemed to smoke.

As if in answer to his question, a white hind whose fawn had died came running up to him as though it had always known him. Giving thanks to God for this miracle, the hermit said to himself, "Well, at least the babies shall not lack for milk."

And so it was that the seven children grew up in the care of the hermit who, though he had vowed to spend his life alone, delighted in their company. He did his best to care for them and to raise them as if they had been his own. They soon learned to call him "Father," for he was all they knew of gentleness and love.

One boy, above all the rest, was especially strong and quick. The hermit named him Hylas, and he soon grew to be a fine hunter. And, if the hermit often wondered where the children had come from, he never spoke of it.

Thus, twelve years passed and, during that time, it seemed that King Orian grew daily weaker and sadder and that, as he did so, Matabrunne grew stronger,

28

until she had all but taken over the governing of the kingdom. Then, one day, a knight in Matabrunne's service, whose name was Savary, happened to see the children playing together in the woods and noticed the silver chains they wore. So beautiful were the children and so bright their silver chains, that Savary hurried back to the castle and poured out his story to Matabrunne. When she heard this, her eyes glittered cruelly.

"Have you told anyone else about this?"

"No, Madam."

"Then take a dozen trusted men," said Matabrunne, "seek out the children with silver chains around their necks and kill them all. Do not fail me. And be sure to bring their chains to me, as proof that they are dead."

Fearful for his life, Savary did as he was bid. But, when he and the men he had gathered to do the evil deed arrived in the clearing near the hermit's hut, they found only six of the children, for the hermit had taken Hylas with him in search of food.

"Six must do," said Savary, grimly, and drew his knife. The children stood fearful and still but, as Savary cut the silver chains from their necks, something strange happened: the children suddenly turned into six beautiful white swans and flew away toward the nearby river.

Fearing for his life, Savary took the six silver chains back to Matabrunne. He told her the seventh had fallen from his pocket somewhere in the forest. Then, trembling, he confessed that the children were still alive, though they had become swans.

But, instead of being angry, the evil queen was well pleased by this news. She took the silver chains to a jeweler and ordered him to melt them down and turn them into a goblet. But when the jeweler set about melting the first chain in his furnace, it grew and grew until there was enough to make two cups. Then the jeweler knew that there was magic at work here. He hid one of the goblets, along with the five remaining chains, and took the other to Matabrunne.

When the jeweler had gone, richly rewarded for his work, Matabrunne poured wine into the goblet and drank a toast to herself. "At last, the power of the silver chains is broken and the children will be swans forever," she said. "Now I have only to rid myself of their mother, and no one will be able to challenge my power."

Then she went to the king and said to him, "My son, it is twelve long years since the evil deed, for which your wife was imprisoned, took place. No evidence has ever been found to show that she was not guilty. It is now your duty to put her to death."

And the king, who seemed to have grown sadder every day since his young queen was put in prison, reluctantly gave his consent. At once, Matabrunne sent messengers to every part of the kingdom to say that the queen was to be burned at the stake for killing her children and that everyone loyal to the king should be there to witness her just punishment.

That night, the old hermit, still perplexed and sad from the loss of the six children, dreamed a dream. In it, he saw the young queen and heard her speaking to him, telling him who the children really were and what had happened to the six who were lost. "Tell my son Hylas the truth and tell him that he alone can save me," she said.

At that, the old hermit awoke with a start and hurried to wake Hylas. When the boy heard what the hermit had dreamed, he declared at once that they must go to the city and rescue his mother.

As they drew near to the city, they saw that a great crowd had already begun to gather to watch the execution. As the king, who had to attend the execution by law, rode through the streets, the boy, Hylas, who had joined the crowd, rushed forward and seized the bridle of his horse. "Who are you?" the boy cried. "And who is that who follows you, in such a sorrowful state?"

"I am the king and that is my queen, who must die for her crimes."

"What proof do you have of those crimes?" demanded Hylas. "It seems to me that you were wrong to accept the word of Matabrunne, for she is a false and wicked woman." All around, the crowd was murmuring and nodding and Matabrunne began to be afraid.

"Do not listen to this insolent child, my son," she said.

But something in the boy's face had caught the king's attention.

"What is your name, child?" he asked.

"My name is Hylas," replied the boy. "And though I am only twelve years old, yet I will take the queen's part. Let anyone who wishes challenge me and I will defend her against these accusations."

"Ha, foolish wretch!" cried Matabrunne. "I have a champion who will soon silence you." And she beckoned to Savary, who came forward unwillingly, not liking to fight so young and untried an opponent.

Hylas was given a horse and armor by one of the king's knights, who also gave him this advice. "Be careful to get up as quickly as you can if you fall. Strike fast and always use the edge of your sword. If you succeed in bringing down your foe, strike hard and show no mercy."

Hylas nodded and was helped onto his horse. He looked small and weak, sitting up high on the steed, though many noticed that he wielded both sword and lance with surprising ease for one so young.

Grimly, Savary lowered his lance and the two charged to meet each other. They met with a crash and both flew from the backs of their horses. Remembering the friendly knight's advice, Hylas sprang to his feet and attacked Savary, who was winded from his fall. In another moment, it was all over. Matabrunne's champion lay dead.

When she saw this, the evil queen tried to flee. But she was quickly caught and brought back to face trial. For now the truth became known, as first Hylas and then his poor mother spoke up. They told what had really happened twelve years since and how there were seven children, of which Hylas himself was one, and how the rest had become swans.

Then the king wept and begged his wife's forgiveness and vowed to punish Matabrunne. Then he joyfully embraced his son.

It was at this moment that the jeweler, whom Matabrunne had employed to make a cup from the silver chains, came forward and told his story. With a cry of joy, the young queen begged him to bring the chains to her and, when he did so, they all went to the nearby river and shook them over the water. At once, six swans came flying toward them and five of them each took one of the chains and became children again. But the sixth, whose chain had been made into the goblet, remained a swan ever after.

Then, amid much weeping both for joy and for sorrow, the king and his young queen and the children went home. The evil Matabrunne was tried and found guilty for her crimes and soon met her end.

As for the seventh swan, it remained always close by on the river, and when Hylas became a knight and rode forth in search of adventure, it went with him, leading him to many wondrous adventures. Because of this, he became known, far and wide, not by his own name, but as the Knight of the Swan.

Everyone was very quiet when Master William finished. Then one of the squires spoke up. "Was Sir Hylas a very brave knight?"

"Oh yes," answered Master William, "You see, he never forgot what had happened to him when he was a boy, how the hermit was so kind to him and how his mother nearly died because of Matabrunne."

"But wasn't he magical, as well?" asked Tom.

"Everyone has a little magic in them," said Master William, slowly. "The important thing is that Hylas treated everyone as equal and saw that no harm ever came to those who asked for his help. Every knight should try to do that, if they can." He stood up. "Now, everyone inside or you'll all be late for supper."

One day, Master William found Tom in the stables, looking up at Sir Brian's great black charger, Gringolet, in his stall.

"Nothing to do?" asked the Armorer. "I'm sure I could find you some harness to clean if you haven't."

The truth of the matter was that Tom was feeling homesick, but he didn't want to admit that.

"Isn't Gringolet marvelous?" he said. "Do you think I will have a horse like him, one day?"

"Perhaps you will," said Master William. "A horse is the most important thing a knight possesses."

"More than his armor?" asked Tom.

"More than his armor or his sword," answered Master William. "Only his honor is more important." He thought for a moment, then said, "Would you like to hear a story about a knight who could lift a horse like this on his shoulders?"

Tom's eyes were as round as coins as he tried to think of anyone being strong enough to lift the great charger. He nodded eagerly.

"This is a story about a famous knight from the land called Rus," began Master William, "and, if you listen carefully, you'll learn that even heroes have a sense of humor."

36

# The Three Journeys of Ilya Murom

A Story from
Russia

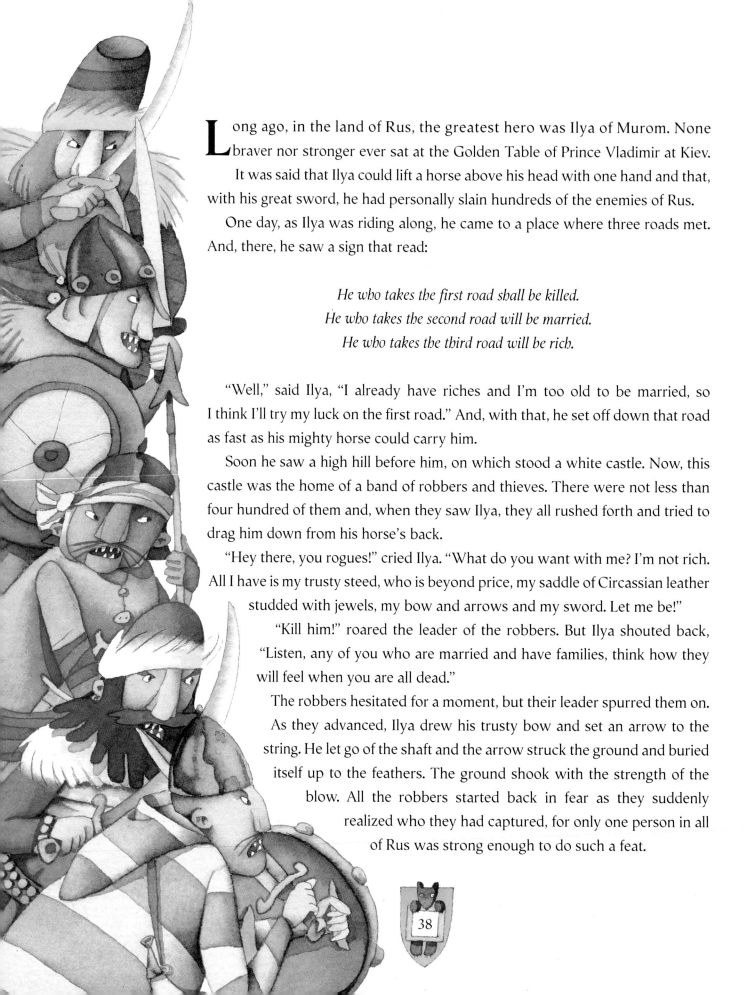

Long ago, in the land of Rus, the greatest hero was Ilya of Murom. None braver nor stronger ever sat at the Golden Table of Prince Vladimir at Kiev.

It was said that Ilya could lift a horse above his head with one hand and that, with his great sword, he had personally slain hundreds of the enemies of Rus.

One day, as Ilya was riding along, he came to a place where three roads met. And, there, he saw a sign that read:

> *He who takes the first road shall be killed.*
> *He who takes the second road will be married.*
> *He who takes the third road will be rich.*

"Well," said Ilya, "I already have riches and I'm too old to be married, so I think I'll try my luck on the first road." And, with that, he set off down that road as fast as his mighty horse could carry him.

Soon he saw a high hill before him, on which stood a white castle. Now, this castle was the home of a band of robbers and thieves. There were not less than four hundred of them and, when they saw Ilya, they all rushed forth and tried to drag him down from his horse's back.

"Hey there, you rogues!" cried Ilya. "What do you want with me? I'm not rich. All I have is my trusty steed, who is beyond price, my saddle of Circassian leather studded with jewels, my bow and arrows and my sword. Let me be!"

"Kill him!" roared the leader of the robbers. But Ilya shouted back, "Listen, any of you who are married and have families, think how they will feel when you are all dead."

The robbers hesitated for a moment, but their leader spurred them on. As they advanced, Ilya drew his trusty bow and set an arrow to the string. He let go of the shaft and the arrow struck the ground and buried itself up to the feathers. The ground shook with the strength of the blow. All the robbers started back in fear as they suddenly realized who they had captured, for only one person in all of Rus was strong enough to do such a feat.

As one man, the robbers fell to their knees.

"Do not kill us, Ilya of Murom!" they cried. "You may take our golden treasure and our herds of fine horses."

Ilya stroked his long beard. "If I take your treasure, I shall have to build vaults to keep it in and, if I take your horses, I shall have to become a herdsman. No, I'm afraid I shall have to kill you."

Then he drew his great long sword and began to lay about him. And wherever he slashed, he cut a swathe as wide as a road. Soon, all the robbers lay dead and Ilya rode back to where the signpost stood at the meeting of the ways and wrote on it:

*Ilya of Murom rode this way and was not killed.*

Then he set off briskly down the second road.

Soon he came to a place too large to be a village and too small to be a town, and there he stopped before a white palace.

At once, a most beautiful lady came forth and smiled at him.

"Welcome, great knight," she said. "Will you not come in? There is food and wine, and soft pillows for your tired head."

"Thank you, my lady," said Ilya, "I don't mind if I do." Then, he went inside and sat down at a great oaken table and was fed with royal amounts of food and drink until he could eat no more and began to yawn prodigiously.

So the lady showed him to a fine room, in which there was a splendid, comfortable-looking bed, and invited him to lie down and sleep. But Ilya guessed that something was not quite right about the lady and, without further ado, he picked her up and dropped her heavily onto the bed. With a scream, she vanished from view, for the bed was but a hollow frame, beneath which lay a pit leading to the dungeons.

Ilya went down into the dark, dank depths below the castle and opened the

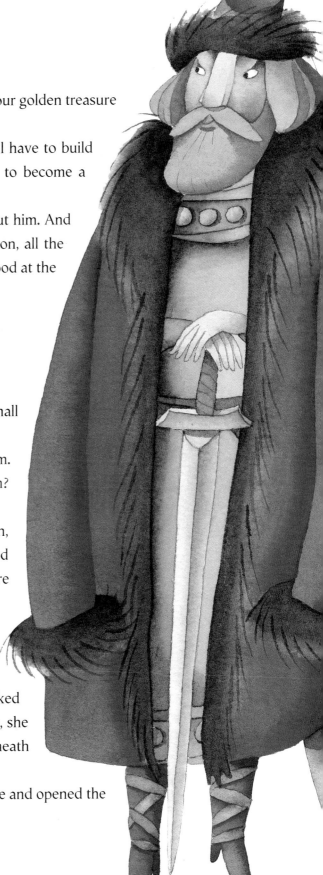

iron gates to the dungeons himself, letting out all the princes and knights and ladies who had fallen foul of the beautiful, but evil, lady. Then, with their thanks still ringing in his ears, he returned once more to the meeting of the ways and wrote on the wooden signpost:

*Ilya of Murom rode this way and was not married.*

Then he set off briskly down the third road.

Far along the way, he came to a huge rock sitting in the middle of the road. It clearly weighed many tons, but Ilya dismounted and set his shoulder against the rock. Giving a mighty heave, he rolled it to one side and there, in a pit, lay gold and jewels and silver and pearls as mighty a hoard as ever you saw.

Ilya looked at it for a while and stroked his long beard. Then he gathered up as much of the treasure as he could and carried it to the nearest town, where he gave it all to be distributed among the poor. With the cries and cheers of the people ringing in his ears, he rode back to the signpost at the meeting of the ways and wrote on it:

*Ilya of Murom rode this way and was not made rich.*

Then, with a laugh, he turned and rode back to the city of Kiev and the rest of the nights of the Golden Table. And, you may be sure, they were greatly entertained by his story, as I hope you were.

**As Master William finished the story, Tom was laughing. "He showed them, didn't he?"**

"He certainly did," said Master William. "But then, he was a real hero. Now, weren't you supposed to be polishing Sir Brian's sword this afternoon?"

"Oh," said Tom, with a guilty look, "I'd forgotten."

"Well, off you go and get it done!" said Master William, his stern look belied by the twinkle in his eyes. "You'll find plenty of clean sand in the armory." He watched as Tom hurried away, all thoughts of homesickness forgotten, and he smiled as he set about his own duties.

"How many of you know what a quest is?" asked Master William, one cold and blustery day.

The boys were gathered around the Armorer in the great hall of the castle, as close to the blazing fire as they could get. Several hands went up. "It means to look for something really hard to find, like the Holy Grail," said one of the pages.

Master William nodded. "Can anyone tell me why one should go on such a quest?"

"To see if they were brave enough?" suggested Tom.

"Well, that's one reason," said Master William, "but you need to be more than brave to succeed on a quest."

"What's more important than courage?" put in one of the older squires.

"Many things," said Master William, "such as being clever enough to know when things are real and when they are tricks. Perronik was clever enough to know the difference and yet everyone thought he was a fool."

"Who's Perronik?" Tom asked.

"Oh, he was a great hero who went on a quest a long time ago," said Master William.

"Tell us about him!" begged the boys.

"Well, I suppose it does show you how people can be mistaken about each other," said the Armorer, slowly. "All right. Listen and I'll tell you how this quest began..."

42

# Perronik the Fool

## A Story from Brittany

Long ago, in the great dark forest of Broceliande, there lived a boy named Perronik. He was, in fact, a very clever fellow, but he was also lazy. He liked nothing so much as hanging about all day, dreaming and gazing up at the sky, as though he expected something wonderful to fall from it. For this reason, everyone called him Perronik the Fool, and swore that no good would ever come of him. But Perronik had a secret dream that he told to no one: he wanted to become a knight.

One day, he knocked at the door of a house that stood just near the edge of the forest. At first the farmer's wife was going to send him away, but Perronik was so full of praise for the wonderful smells coming from her oven that she softened and gave him a crust of dry bread and a scraping of bacon fat.

At that moment, there was a clatter of hooves and a tall knight on a black horse rode up. "Can you tell me the way to the Castle of Kerglas?" he asked.

The woman turned pale. "Why ever would you want to go there?" she cried. "It's a terrible place. The evil sorcerer, Sir Rogier, lives there."

"I know all about that," said the knight, "but I am seeking the Golden Basin and the Adamantine Spear that he keeps in his castle. The basin can bring the dead to life and the spear kills everything it touches."

The woman shivered. "No one ever comes back from that place," she said.

"Indeed, they don't," said the knight, "but no one else has had the benefit of advice from the Hermit of Blavet."

"What did the hermit tell you?" asked Perronik, who had been listening to all this with wider and wider eyes.

"He told me everything I had to do to overcome the spells the sorcerer has set around his castle. First, I must ride through this dark forest, where all kinds of wizardry will be turned against me. Then, I must find a certain apple tree and take one of its apples. But to do that, I have to overcome a dwarf with a weapon that burns everything it touches to ashes."

44

"And after that?" demanded Perronik.

"Oh, nothing much," replied the knight, boastfully. "Then I must find the flower that laughs, which is guarded by a lion with a mane of serpents. I must pick the flower and make my way to a river where I will find a lady dressed in black. I must take her on my horse to the Castle of Kerglas where she will tell me what to do next."

The farmer's wife tried her best to persuade the knight not to go, but he only shook his head and said that knights were bound by honor to go on the most dangerous quests they could find. Then he rode off in a cloud of dust.

At that moment, the farmer came home, looking gloomy. "I've had to send that boy who looks after the cows away," he said. "He's just no use at all." Then he spotted Perronik, who was leaning against the wall with a faraway look in his eyes. "I don't suppose you want a job?" he asked. Perronik was really too lazy to want any kind of job, but he could still taste the bread and bacon fat on his tongue, so he nodded.

So Perronik became a cowherd. All day long, he watched to see that the farmer's cattle did not stray too far into the forest. And, truth to tell, he found the job very dull — though it did leave him plenty of time for dreaming of becoming a knight.

Then, one day, he heard the sound of hooves on the track and saw a huge, dark figure on a wild, black horse riding by. As soon as he saw him, Perronik knew that he must be Sir Rogier, the Sorcerer of Kerglas, because he carried a dark and gleaming spear in one hand, the tip of which shone with unearthly light, and around his neck hung a golden basin. Following him was a yearling foal, which tossed its head and rolled its eyes as though it was afraid.

Next day, as Perronik was herding the cows, he saw a tall man with a white beard standing in the road.

"Are you looking for the way to Kerglas?" he asked the man.

"Why should I do that, since I know the way better than most?" answered the stranger.

"You have been there?" cried Perronik, wide-eyed. "How is it you are still alive?"

"Because Sir Rogier has nothing to fear from me," laughed the man. "I am his brother and a sorcerer like him. When I want to get to Kerglas, I simply make a spell to call a young foal my brother has. It knows the way better than anything and soon takes me there."

As Perronik looked on in wonder, the man drew three circles in the earth, muttered some strange words and then said aloud:

> *"Foal light of foot,*
> *Foal sharp of tooth,*
> *Foal, I am here,*
> *Come where I wait."*

At once, the little horse appeared and the sorcerer's brother put a halter on it and rode away into the forest.

Perronik thought and thought about this meeting. He remembered everything the knight had said about how to get to Kerglas and how to survive the magic of the evil sorcerer. He began to plan how he could defeat Sir Rogier and all the other strange people the knight had described.

First, he made a halter of brown hemp and a snare for catching snipe. Then he got a linen bag and filled it with birdlime and larks' feathers. Last, he took a piece of hard bread and rubbed it all over with bacon fat.

With everything ready, Perronik scattered breadcrumbs along the road where the sorcerer used to ride every day. Then he hid in some bushes until Sir Rogier came along on his wild black horse, with the foal trotting behind. From his hiding place, Perronik watched Sir Rogier go by. The foal smelled the bread smeared with bacon fat and stopped to eat it, but the sorcerer soon passed out of sight. Quick as a flash, Perronik jumped out and put the halter on the foal. Then he jumped onto its back and let it go wherever it liked, for he was certain it would take him to Kerglas.

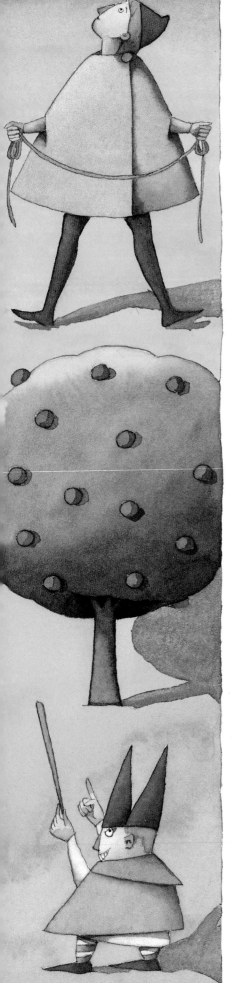

Sure enough, the foal ran as fast as it could toward the castle. As it went through the forest, all the magic spells of protection placed there by the evil sorcerer began to work. Cracks appeared in the earth, spouting flames. Streams became raging rivers when Perronik came near them. Huge boulders broke away from the hillsides and came crashing down where he rode. But Perronik knew these things were not real. They were only tricks, so he pulled his cap over his eyes and clung on to the foal's neck as hard as he could, waiting for his ordeal to end.

At last, they left the dark forest and came to a meadow, where there grew an enormous apple tree with its branches loaded down with fruit. In front of it stood a dwarf and, in his hand, he held the fiery weapon that turned everything it touched to ashes. When he saw Perronik, he gave a loud cry and rushed forward.

Perronik raised his hat and said, "Please don't let me disturb you. I only want to pass by here on my way to the Castle of Kerglas. Sir Rogier has asked me to come."

"And who might you be?" said the dwarf, suspiciously.

"I am the master's new servant," said Perronik. "You know, the one he is waiting for."

"I know of no such thing," answered the dwarf. "You look like a trickster to me."

"I am nothing of the kind," replied Perronik, as innocently as he knew how. "I'm just a bird-catcher and trainer. Anyway," he added, "you can see this is the master's horse I am riding. That's how urgently he needs me."

"Humph!" said the dwarf. "I want to see you catch a bird. They are always eating the fruit of my apple tree. Set up your snare. If you catch a bird, I'll let you pass."

Perronik agreed. He tied one end of the snare to the tree, then he called the dwarf to hold the other while he set up the lures. Then, quick as a wink, he pulled the snare tight and the dwarf was caught!

Screaming with fury, the dwarf struggled to free himself. But, as hard as he pulled, the snare only grew tighter and, in the end, he could not move at all. Perronik, meanwhile, picked the largest apple he could see on the tree, got back on the foal and rode on as fast as he could.

Soon he came to the most wonderful gardens he had ever seen. There were flowers too rich and rare to name and all kinds of herbs and ornamental trees. But, most wonderful of all, was the magical flower the knight had told him of, which laughed gently as it nodded above the other blossoms on a long stalk.

As he was looking in wonder at all this, a huge lion with a mane of serpents and eyes like mill wheels came racing toward him. Perronik quickly doffed his cap and wished the lion and his family every good thing he could think of. Then he asked if he was on the right road to Kerglas.

Surprised by this greeting, for he was used to people running away in terror, the lion roared: "What do you want in Kerglas?"

"With your permission, Sir Lion," said Perronik, "I am in the service of a great lady who wants to send a gift to Sir Rogier."

"What gift?" demanded the lion.

"Why, lark pie," replied Perronik.

"Larks," said the lion, licking its teeth. "It's been centuries since I tasted larks. Do you have any with you?"

"Oh, yes, as many as I can get in this bag," said Perronik, holding up the bag filled with feathers and birdlime.

"Let me see," said the lion.

"But if I open the bag, the larks will fly away," said Perronik. "Then Sir Rogier will be angry and probably kill me."

"Just open the bag far enough for me to look in," said the lion.

Perronik did just that and the lion thrust its head right into the bag. There, it found itself caught up in the feathers and birdlime and, quick as a wink, Perronik drew the cord tight around its neck, so that it was completely unable to escape. Then he ran to the laughing flower, picked it and hurried on his way as fast as he could.

49

50

Soon he saw the grim walls of the Castle of Kerglas. A swift river ran before it, beside which was a meadow. There, Perronik saw a lady, dressed all in black. As he came up close to her, he saw that her face was yellow. "Do you wish to cross the river?" he asked her politely.

The lady nodded. "That is why I am waiting for you," she said. "Only your horse knows the safe place to cross."

So the lady climbed up behind Perronik and they crossed the river in a moment. As they reached the further side, the lady said, "Do you know who I am?"

"I would guess that you must be a very noble and powerful lady indeed," said Perronik.

"Noble I am, since my lineage stretches back thousands of years. Powerful I must be, since everyone fears me."

"What is your name, great lady?"

"I am called Plague," she said.

At once, Perronik jumped down and tried to run away. But the lady called after him. "Do not be afraid. I have not come for you, it is Sir Rogier I want."

"But, surely, he is a sorcerer and therefore cannot die," said Perronik.

"Normally, that would be true," said the lady. "But the apple you have comes from a magical tree. If you can get the evil sorcerer to eat some, he will become mortal and can therefore die."

"I will try," said Perronik, "but, if Sir Rogier is killed, how will I find the Golden Basin and the Adamantine Spear? They are locked in a deep, dark dungeon under the castle and only the sorcerer can open the door."

"The laughing flower, which you carry, can open all doors and its light will shine in even the darkest place," the lady replied.

Perronik had to be satisfied with this and so they went on together to the castle. There they found the evil sorcerer, stretched out at his ease under a canopy of silk.

"That is my foal you are riding!" roared Sir Rogier.

"So it is, oh greatest of sorcerers," replied Perronik.

"How did you overcome the magic spells in the forest?" the sorcerer demanded.

"Why, I said the words your brother taught to me," Perronik replied. "When I came to the edge of the forest, I said:

*Foal light of foot,*
*Foal sharp of tooth,*
*Foal, I am here,*
*Come where I wait."*

"So you know my brother," said Sir Rogier.

"As well as any servant knows his master," replied Perronik.

"Then why has he sent you to me?"

"He wanted you to have two rare and wonderful gifts: this apple of joy and this lady. If you eat the apple, you will never feel discontented again and, if you take this lady into your house, there will be nothing left for you to wish for on this earth."

"Give me the apple, then," said the sorcerer, greedily, "and let the lady enter my house." Then he bit into the fruit.

At once, Lady Plague touched him and the evil sorcerer fell dead. Perronik hurried into the castle, passing through a hundred halls, each one finer than the last, until he reached the dungeons. There, before him, was a silver gate, firmly locked. But as soon as he held up the flower that laughed, the door opened and there, before him, were the Golden Basin and the Adamantine Spear, the tip of which shone with an unearthly light. Perronik snatched them up and ran out of the castle as quickly as he could. Hardly had he left it when he heard the greatest crashing and thundering and, when he looked back, he saw the Castle of Kerglas falling into ruins.

Perronik hurried on until he reached the great city of Nantes, where the king lived. There he used the Golden Basin and the Adamantine Spear to perform many great deeds. The king made him a knight, just as he had always wanted, and, in time, he inherited the kingdom and ruled long and wisely. There are those who say that, thanks to the Golden Basin, Perronik is living still. But others are just as sure that the sorcerer's brother got back the magical objects and that, if anyone wants to find them, they must go and look for them.

"So you see," said Master William, "if you really want to be good knights, you have to keep on trying, even if you think it's never going to happen. Perronik wasn't really that brave — at least, he wasn't to begin with. But he wanted to be a knight so much that he overcame his fears."

"And he knew the things in the forest were tricks," Tom pointed out.

"Yes. Sometimes, as I said, that can be more important than being brave," said Master William. He looked up toward one of the long, narrow windows that pierced the huge walls of the hall. "Well," he said, "I think it's starting to snow."

With cries of delight, the boys scattered from the hall in a moment, all thoughts of quests and chivalry forgotten, in the rush to be the first to see the white flakes falling on the castle courtyard. Master William got up more slowly, then went, smiling, after them.

53

"Why so gloomy, Tom?" asked Master William. "Your face is as long as a rainy day." They were sitting together in the armory, using a special fine sand to scrub clean Sir Brian's armor and making sure there was not a single spot of rust on it anywhere.

Tom frowned. "My brother, Robert, is going to be knighted next week," he said.

"Surely, that is reason to be happy," replied Master William.

"But he always gets to do everything first!" Tom complained. "Just because he's older than me."

Master William was silent for awhile, scrubbing at a particularly stubborn spot on his master's armor. Then he said, "You know, a lot of great knights had older brothers and some of them felt just as you do. But, in the end, some of them became more famous than their brothers."

"Really?" Tom exclaimed.

Master William nodded. "I remember a story about a great knight from the East, who learned a lot from being a younger son."

Tom put down the piece of armor he was cleaning. "Tell me about him, please," he said.

54

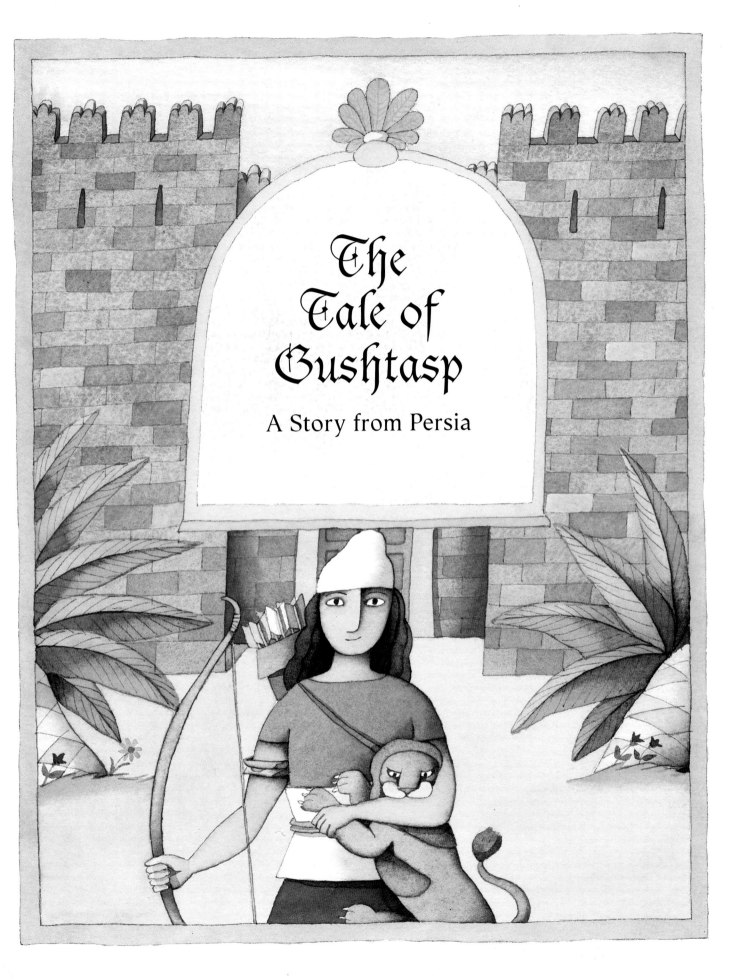

Long ago, in the ancient land of Persia, there was a king named Lohrasp who had two sons, Zarir and Gushtasp. Both were clever, brave young men, skilled in swordplay and horsemanship. But King Lohrasp preferred Zarir, his elder son, lavishing many gifts upon him, while almost ignoring his younger son, Gushtasp.

For many years, Gushtasp said nothing about this but, one day, he could bear it no longer. He went to the king and spoke to him, in the presence of the whole court: "Lord King, I am your son and I have served you well all my life. Now, just as the great King Khosroes before you, I beg that you name me your successor and grant that I may serve you even better."

King Lohrasp was silent for a moment. Then he said, "My son, you are over-eager, and that is not a good thing in one so nobly born. Given time, you shall be recognized but, for now, you must bide your time."

Then, remembering all the service he had given to his father and, even more, the many gifts and favors granted to his brother, Gushtasp said angrily, "Sire, if you have neither love nor recognition to offer me, your own son, then I shall seek for both elsewhere!" So saying, he strode from the court. Leaving all his wealth and fine clothes behind in favor of a simple robe, he saddled his horse and rode forth that very night, with but a little gold and without his usual servants and bodyguards.

For many months, Gushtasp wandered through the lands ruled over by his father. But, in time, he came to the border of his great kingdom and crossed into the Empire of the Lands of the West, governed by the great Caesar. And, having heard much of that fabled country, Gushtasp set out for the great city of Rome, which some men called the Center of the World.

When he arrived in Rome, Gushtasp saw that it was, indeed, among the most wondrous places he had ever seen and so he decided to stay there for a time. After finding lodgings, he went in search of employment, for the gold he had brought with him from his father's court was almost gone.

First, he went to a scrivener, who copied out letters and documents for those who could not write. "Sir," said Gushtasp, "I am a scribe from Persia. If you were to make me your assistant, you would not find me lazy."

The scrivener looked at Gushtasp's powerful muscles and strong hands.

57

"You were made to wear armor and carry a sword," he said. "There is no work for you here."

Gushtasp shrugged and went on his way, until he found a horse dealer. "Sir," he said, "I am an excellent rider and I can tame any horse you give me. If you put me in charge of your herds, you will not regret it."

"I don't doubt that all you say is true," replied the horse dealer. "But I do not know you at all and so I would be foolish to put you in charge of my herds. For all I know, you could be a thief."

Gushtasp sighed and went on his way. This time, he sought out a camel driver. "Sir," he said, "I ask no wages. For just my keep, I will gladly join those who care for your camels."

The camel driver looked closely at Gushtasp. "Despite your poor dress, you have the manners of one nobly born. I am only a simple man, I could not offer work to such as you."

By now, Gushtasp was beginning to get desperate. He went next to a smithy and begged the smith to make him an apprentice. The smith looked at Gushtasp's broad shoulders and muscular arms and said, cautiously, "You might make a good apprentice, at that. But before I take you on, I want to see if you are strong enough for the work." So he ordered two of his assistants to take a ball of iron from the furnace and to place it on the anvil. Then he gave Gushtasp

a hammer and told him to flatten the ball of white-hot metal into a disc.

Gushtasp took the hammer and went to it with a will. But a single blow flattened the iron ball — and broke the anvil beneath it!

"Away with you!" cried the smith. "There is no work here for someone who would quickly reduce my smithy to ruins!"

Gushtasp threw down the hammer and went on his way, wondering where he would sleep that night and whether he would be able to get anything to eat. His footsteps led him through one of the great gates of the city to a shady place beneath a great tree. There he sat, head in hands, wondering if he had been wise to leave the comforts of his father's court where he had servants to look after his every need.

Now, it happened that an elder of the city passed by on his way home. When he saw Gushtasp, sitting forlornly under the tree, he went up to him. "You look as though you have all the troubles of the world on your shoulders," he said. "If it would be helpful to come home with me and talk about what is troubling you, you are most welcome."

Gushtasp thanked the good old man and went home with him. There he remained for some time as an honored guest. He told his host nothing of his true name and identity, merely saying that he was from Persia and that his name was Farukzad.

Now, it happened that at this time, one of Caesar's daughters, whose name was Katayun, came of age and Caesar decided it was time for her to marry. He called together all the elders of Rome (among them Gushtasp's host) and then summoned Katayun to choose one of them to be her husband.

She walked all around the hall, looking at every man there. But, after she had done this, Katayun shook her head and said, "Lord father, I can see no man here whom I would wish to marry."

Frowning, Caesar sent the elders away, instructing them to send all the young and noble men to the palace the next day, so that his daughter might choose one of them to marry.

When he returned home, Gushtasp's host told him what had happened at the court. "Why not," he said, "present yourself tomorrow?"

"But I am poor — and a foreigner," replied Gushtasp. "I am hardly the sort of person who could marry Caesar's daughter."

"As to that," replied the elder, "I know nothing of your birth or station in life, but you are well-spoken, handsome and strong. I believe you have as good a chance as anyone to succeed in capturing this maiden's heart."

So the next day, Gushtasp went and stood in line with all the other suitors but, when he entered the hall, he stood apart from them in a corner.

Presently, Katayun arrived with her women attendants and began to walk about the court, staring into the face of every young man who was there. Not one of them sparked any interest in her. Finally, with a sigh, she asked her maidens if she had seen everyone.

"All save one," answered her attendants, "but he is so poorly dressed, he is not worthy of your attention."

"Nevertheless, I shall see him," said Katayun firmly. She made her way over to where Gushtasp stood and she looked into his eyes. Whatever she saw there made her smile and, turning to her father, she said, "This is the man I shall marry."

When he learned that his daughter had chosen a penniless foreigner, Caesar was very angry. "If you marry this man, you will get neither a blessing nor a dowry from me!" he shouted. "Nor will either of you be welcome at my court."

Katayun bowed her head sadly, but she had made up her mind. Gushtasp, too, was more than happy, for he had fallen in love with Katayun the moment their eyes had met. They were married that same day and went to live with the elder, who had done so much to help the young stranger.

In the years that followed, Gushtasp and Katayun were happy together and, in that time, the young knight proved himself in every way to be as noble in nature as any of the youths of Rome. In the end, Caesar recognized his good qualities and summoned his daughter and her husband back to his court.

Soon after that, it happened that Caesar began to look toward the Empire of Persia with thoughts of conquest. He sent a message to King Lohrasp, demanding that he should pay tribute to Rome or suffer the consequences. Then he gathered a huge army and set up camp on Persian soil, hoping in this way to frighten Lohrasp into submission. With him went Gushtasp.

When the Persian king heard of Caesar's demands, he was greatly angered. Yet he knew that Caesar was powerful and so he hesitated to drag his people into a long war. He decided to send his eldest son, Zarir, to meet with the Roman leader in the hope that, through diplomacy, war might be avoided.

When Zarir arrived at the Roman camp, he was taken to Caesar, who was sitting on a great golden throne before his war tent. Beside him, on a small throne was sitting Gushtasp, dressed in Roman fashion.

When Zarir saw Gushtasp, he could not help but stare, because he thought it might be his brother. He was not sure, because it had been many years since he had seen him. But Gushtasp did not make any sign of recognition.

Zarir greeted Caesar proudly. "The king, my father, bids you depart in peace, or else meet him in the field of war."

Caesar frowned. "Why do you not greet my son?" he demanded.

"Sir, I have nothing to say to a runaway slave," answered Zarir, coldly.

Caesar gave a puzzled look at Gushtasp. Then he said to Zarir, "We have nothing more to say to each other. It shall be war." And he dismissed the prince with a wave of his hand.

When Zarir had withdrawn stiffly, Caesar asked Gushtasp, "You are Persian and you have told me you were once at the king's court. Why did you not speak with the prince?"

"Sir," answered Gushtasp, "it seemed to me that I should not do so. Yet, I was indeed once respected at the court of King Lohrasp and I do not think my people want this war. Let me go and speak with the king. It may be that I can avert the conflict to come."

To this, Caesar agreed and Gushtasp set off at once for his father's court. When Lohrasp saw his long-lost son, his joy knew no bounds. For, truly, he had long doubted his actions in preferring Zarir. When he heard the story of Gushtasp's adventures and that he was married to Caesar's daughter, the king began to speak of giving up his throne and setting Gushtasp in his place.

Gushtasp bowed his head before his father and begged him to avert the imminent war. To this, King Lohrasp agreed and Gushtasp sent word to Caesar, explaining everything.

When he heard that his son-in-law would soon be king of Persia, Caesar at once agreed to withdraw his army. Peace soon followed and, not long after, Gushtasp was crowned. With Katayun at his side, he ruled happily for a long time and brought good fortune to both empires. But Gushtasp never forgot his adventures as a young man and, ever after, encouraged the young knights of his court to seek honor, wherever they could, be it in Persia or elsewhere in the wide world.

"That's a wonderful story," cried Tom. "I specially love the bit where Gushtasp tries all those different jobs."

Master William smiled. "And you see how even younger sons can do well for themselves," he said.

"Yes," agreed Tom. Then he jumped up. "I'm going to send a message to Robert right away, wishing him good luck at the ceremony."

"Don't forget to finish that piece of armor you're cleaning first," said Master William.

Master William came upon Tom and Hubert fighting each other in the grassy field behind the castle walls. Nearby lay two sets of bows and arrows and a big, heavy, straw-stuffed target.

"What's all this about?" demanded Master William, pulling the boys apart.

"I wanted to do some archery practice," panted Tom angrily, "but he wouldn't set up the target."

"Well, why should I?" yelled Hubert. "I wanted to shoot the arrows as well. He wouldn't fetch the target!"

"Now, listen," said Master William, firmly. "It takes two people to carry that target and two to set it up. Why didn't you do it together? That way, you would both have been able to shoot at it."

The two boys fell silent, looking sheepish.

Master William turned and easily picked up the heavy target, setting it up on its stand. "Now," he said, "let there be no more fighting, or I won't tell you the story of the knight from a far land who learned to cooperate with some very unusual warriors."

Both boys turned and gave him their full attention.

# Yogodayu and the Army of Bees

A story from Japan

A long time ago, in the ancient land of Japan, there lived a great *samurai* warrior named Yogodayu. Having made a name and fortune for himself in the service of the emperor, he retired to a wild and desolate place called Yamoto. There he built himself a small fortress, garrisoned with his own personal army.

Now it happened that Yogodayu fell out with his brother-in-law, who was himself a powerful warlord. One day, this warrior launched a surprise attack against Yogodayu and, in the battle that followed, only a handful of Yogodayu's men escaped with their lives.

They fled from the battlefield and hid in a cave in the mountains for two days, until Yogodayu was sure no one was coming after them. Then, he came out and looked about him, cautiously. There was no sign of their enemies, but he happened to see a large bee caught in a spider's web and, with gentle hands, he set the creature free, saying to it, "Ah, little warrior, fly back to your hive! It is a pleasure to set a trapped thing free. I only wish I might do the same for myself and my soldiers."

The bee flew off at once but that night, as he lay on his rough bed in the cave, Yogodayu dreamed a wonderful dream. A *samurai* clad in black and yellow came and stood before him. "Sir," he said, "I wish to help you, as you helped me."

"Who are you?" asked Yogodayu.

"I am the bee you helped to escape," replied the other. "I am more grateful than you can imagine and so I have devised a plan to help you overthrow your enemies and regain your fortune."

"How can I do that when I am so outnumbered?" asked Yogodayu.

"Ah," replied the bee, "I will see to that. Here is what you must do. Gather as many men as you can and get them all to bring jars and containers. Then, build a wooden house at the entrance of the valley below here and let it be known that you are assembling an army to attack your brother-in-law. Leave the rest to me. Be assured that you will not fail to win against your enemies."

With that, Yogodayu woke up. At once, he set about doing what the bee had told him. He sent several of his most trusted men to gather others, who would fight alongside them. All of them were to bring back jars and other kinds of containers.

The warriors soon returned and now Yogodayu ordered them to build a wooden house at the entrance to the valley below. When they had done this, they placed all

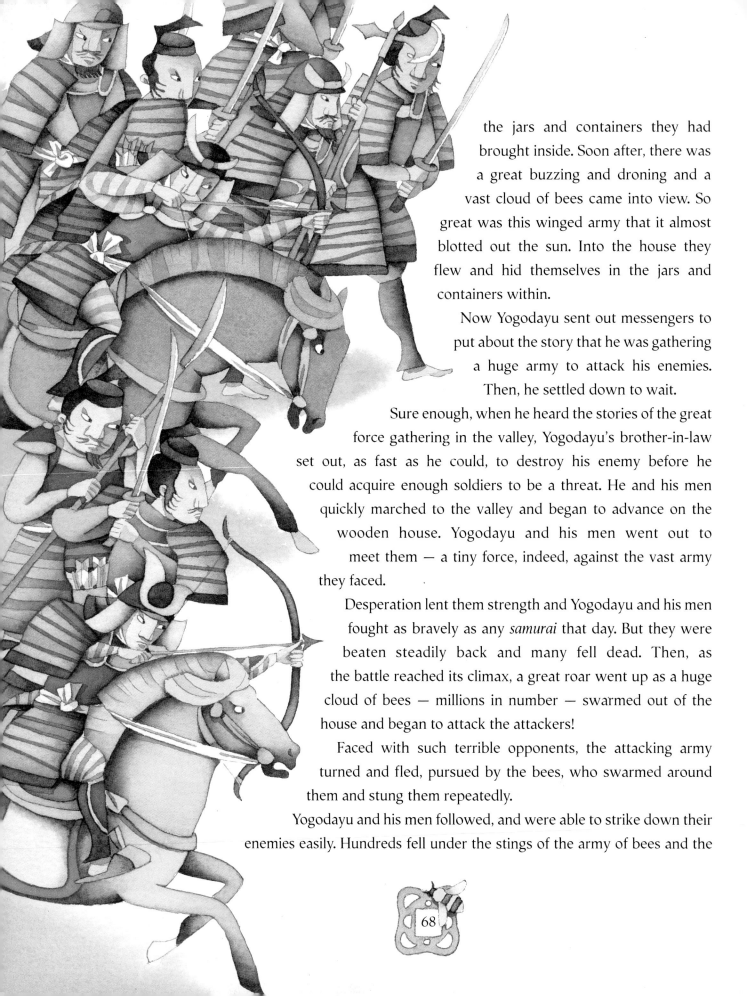

the jars and containers they had brought inside. Soon after, there was a great buzzing and droning and a vast cloud of bees came into view. So great was this winged army that it almost blotted out the sun. Into the house they flew and hid themselves in the jars and containers within.

Now Yogodayu sent out messengers to put about the story that he was gathering a huge army to attack his enemies. Then, he settled down to wait.

Sure enough, when he heard the stories of the great force gathering in the valley, Yogodayu's brother-in-law set out, as fast as he could, to destroy his enemy before he could acquire enough soldiers to be a threat. He and his men quickly marched to the valley and began to advance on the wooden house. Yogodayu and his men went out to meet them — a tiny force, indeed, against the vast army they faced.

Desperation lent them strength and Yogodayu and his men fought as bravely as any *samurai* that day. But they were beaten steadily back and many fell dead. Then, as the battle reached its climax, a great roar went up as a huge cloud of bees — millions in number — swarmed out of the house and began to attack the attackers!

Faced with such terrible opponents, the attacking army turned and fled, pursued by the bees, who swarmed around them and stung them repeatedly.

Yogodayu and his men followed, and were able to strike down their enemies easily. Hundreds fell under the stings of the army of bees and the swords of Yogodayu's warriors. At the end of the day, most of his brother-in-law's army lay dead, and Yogodayu marched at the head of his small force to retake the fortress that he had but recently lost.

Afterward, Yogodayu ordered all of the dead bees to be gathered up and buried beneath a shady tree, close by the castle. Nor did he ever forget the help he had received from the bees. Indeed, he built a small shrine to them and, in later years, he would often go there to honor the spirits of the little black and yellow soldiers of the army of bees.

"So you see," said Master William, "if Yogodayu had not trusted the bees, he would probably never have regained his lands. Being a knight isn't just about being strong enough to do things on your own. Sometimes you need to cooperate with each other."

"And if Yogodayu hadn't set free that bee in the first place, the other bees wouldn't have helped him," added Tom.

"Exactly," said Master William. He stood up. "Now, if you two are going to get in any archery practice before sunset, you'd better get started."

As he walked away, he could hear the satisfying plunk of arrows hitting the target and the cries of "Good shot!" from both boys, their anger forgotten in their delight at each other's skill.

The first snows were already thick on the ground and decorating the tops of the castle walls. Christmas was only a few weeks away and already there was an air of excitement in the great building. Sir Brian had invited a great many guests for the festival. There was to be hunting and even a tournament, in which visiting knights would join in friendly mock battle with each other to prove who was the strongest. Among them would be Tom's father and his brother, Robert, who had been knighted only a few months before.

Tom was almost beside himself with excitement and, as for the rest of the squires and pages, they had a hard time concentrating on any of their instruction. Several times, Master William had to break up squabbles between them, mostly provoked by sheer excitement. Finally, he could stand it no longer.

"Listen to me," he said one morning. "If you can get all your chores and lessons done today without fighting with each other, I'll tell you a story about the knight who loved Christmas so much, he couldn't wait for the year to pass. And that got him into a lot of trouble!"

The boys looked at each other and, after that, there was peace around the castle for the rest of the day as they applied themselves industriously to their tasks. As dusk fell, they gathered in the warm and smoky armory and Master William, a tankard of frothy ale at his side, began his tale...

# Sir Cliges
# and the
# Cherry Tree

## A Story from France

There was once a knight named Sir Cliges, who loved to celebrate Christmas more than anything else. Every December, he held a great feast to which he invited everyone in the neighborhood who wished to come. There was food enough for all, with plenty of wine and sweetmeats. No one went away without a generous gift of some kind — a horse perhaps, a warm cloak or even a gold ring. Whatever he could afford — and sometimes more — Sir Cliges gave.

But, as the years went by, he spent so much money that he had almost none left. Even so, Sir Cliges would not hear of abandoning his usual custom. He decided to pledge several of his manor houses in order to raise enough money to give one more splendid feast, fully believing that he would soon redeem them.

That year, Sir Cliges' Christmas feast was as generous as ever but, when it was over and the new year had dawned, he found that all his money was gone and that he had few possessions left. He was forced to move with his family into one small house and send many of their old servants away.

So the year passed and soon it was almost time for Christmas again. Sir Cliges heard that King Uther Pendragon was going to hold a splendid feast of his own in a nearby city. Every highborn man and woman in the realm was invited — all except for Sir Cliges, whom the king believed to be dead, so long was it since he had last heard from him.

Sir Cliges was terribly sad. Not only could he no longer afford to celebrate the holy day as he had always done, but he could not even go to the king's feast. Instead, he was forced to stand at the window and listen to the distant sounds of merrymaking carried on the wind from behind the walls of the city. With tears in his eyes, Sir Cliges prayed aloud to God to forgive him for not celebrating the birthday of His Son in a fitting manner.

Then, Sir Cliges' wife begged him not to be so sad. "Today is no day to grieve, husband. We have meat on the table and good wine to drink. Our children are well and healthy and so are we. Come now, let us enjoy ourselves."

And Sir Cliges smiled and hid his sorrow. He spent the day happily enough with his wife and their two children, making sport and playing games with them, until night fell.

The next day, Sir Cliges and his family went to church and the knight prayed that, whatever happened to him, his family should be spared all hardship. And his lady prayed that her husband should find peace and contentment and put away his sorrows.

When Mass was ended, they went home and Sir Cliges wandered into the little garden where he loved to sit on sunny summer days. Now, in the middle of winter, it was white with snow, and icicles hung from the trees. Sir Cliges knelt down beneath a cherry tree that used to give sweet-smelling shade from the sun and thanked God for his family and for the poverty which had come to them. "For," he said, "I truly believe it was pride that led me to hold such splendid feasts and thus to spend all the fortune I possessed."

As he knelt there in the snow, one of the branches of the cherry tree broke off and struck him on the shoulder. Sir Cliges looked at it in wonder, and saw that it had green leaves and fruit upon it, as fresh as in the season of summer.

"What kind of tree bears fruit in the middle of winter?" he cried. Then he took some of the cherries and ate them; and they were as sweet as any he had ever tasted. Excitedly, Sir Cliges hurried inside to show the cherries to his wife.

"See what a marvel I have found in our garden!" he exclaimed.

The lady was as astonished as he had been. "Husband," she said, "let us gather some more of this miraculous fruit and take it to the king in the city. Surely, he will reward you for such a wonderful gift."

So Sir Cliges went out and gathered as much of the fruit as he could and, the next day, he set out for the city. He had to walk, since he had been forced to sell his horse and armor. Instead, he took a sturdy staff for support and carried with him a basket filled with cherries.

Sir Cliges soon reached the gates of the city, which was full of people who had come to catch a glimpse of the king and his courtiers on this great occasion. At the entrance to the hall, where the feasting was to take place, was a porter whose job it was to keep out troublesome people. He took one look at the knight in his rough clothes and homespun cloak and told him to join a line of beggars who were waiting to receive the gifts that the king traditionally gave out at this time of year.

But Sir Cliges held his ground and spoke up firmly. "See," he said, "I have brought a gift for the king, such as only God could provide."

The porter peered, suspiciously, into the basket. When he saw the cherries, his eyes gleamed greedily. "I'll let you in," he replied, "providing you promise to give me a third of whatever the king gives you."

Sir Cliges agreed and was allowed to enter the hall. There he met the Royal Usher, who raised his staff of office and threatened to have him thrown out. But again, Sir Cliges held his ground and, opening the basket, allowed the usher to look inside.

When the usher saw the sparkle of the fruit and smelled its rich smell, he agreed to admit the poor knight, but only on condition that he promise to give a third of whatever the king gave him in return. Again, Sir Cliges agreed and was allowed to pass.

Now he met a third man, the king's High Steward, and everything happened just as before. The man was about to throw Sir Cliges out but, when he saw what was in the basket, he agreed to let the knight pass, if he promised to give the steward a third of whatever bounty the king gave.

Sir Cliges sighed for he saw that, whatever good might come of his gift, he had lost it all between the three greedy men. But he nodded all the same and was allowed to go forward.

Sir Cliges knelt before the king and uncovered the basket. "Sire," he said, "I bring you a gift this Christmas, which is surely from Heaven itself."

The king took the basket and looked into it in wonder. "This is indeed a marvelous gift," he said. Then he told Sir Cliges — whom he did not recognize — to sit at one of the long tables that stretched down both sides of the hall and to join in the feasting.

And so Sir Cliges, who was too proud to remind the king that he had once been one of his own knights, went to sit down at the table and the feast began. And very fine it was, with stuffed swans and pheasant and roasted pigs and quails and much, much more. When it was over, the king beckoned Sir Cliges to come near him.

"That was truly one of the finest gifts I have ever been given," he said. "What kind of reward would you like in return?"

Sir Cliges had been thinking deeply about this throughout the feast. Now he said, "Sire, I ask only that you give me three blows and the right to distribute them as I think fit."

The king frowned. "I never heard of such a request," he said. "This seems to me to be a very poor jest. Ask me for something else."

But Sir Cliges stubbornly refused to change his mind and, in the end, with a shake of his head, the king agreed, reluctantly giving Sir Cliges three light blows to the head.

Then, Sir Cliges went through the hall seeking the porter, the usher and the steward.

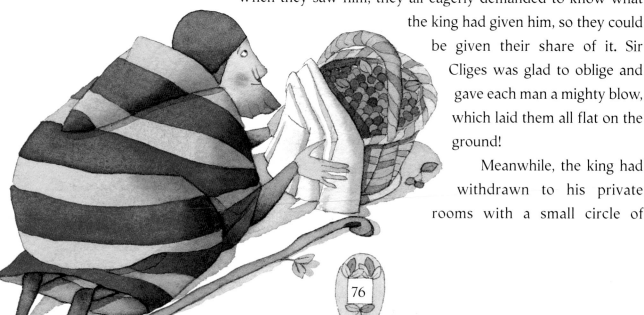

When they saw him, they all eagerly demanded to know what the king had given him, so they could be given their share of it. Sir Cliges was glad to oblige and gave each man a mighty blow, which laid them all flat on the ground!

Meanwhile, the king had withdrawn to his private rooms with a small circle of friends and was enjoying himself with much music and mirth. And it happened that a minstrel sang a ballad about Sir Cliges. As he listened, the king began to wonder what had happened to the good knight, who once was a frequent visitor to his court. When the minstrel had finished, the king asked if he knew anything about the man of whose deeds he sang.

The minstrel shook his head. "Nay, sire," he said. "All I know is that he is much missed hereabouts by all who celebrate Christmas. I hear he has left the country."

"That is a pity," said the king. "He was a good and brave man, and I wish that I might see him again."

Sir Cliges, who had been standing near and heard this, came and knelt before the king and thanked him for the gift of the three blows.

The king looked at him in wonder, and asked how he had meant to use the gift. Then, Sir Cliges told him the whole story and how he had given out the blows to the porter, the usher and the steward.

When he heard this, the king laughed out loud. "By my faith," he said, "tell me your name, for I like you well."

"Sire," said Sir Cliges, "I am Sir Cliges, who was formerly your knight."

The king was amazed to hear this and bade the knight sit down with him. When he heard how his old friend had fallen upon hard times because of his generosity to others, he ordered his coffers to be opened and gave back all the goods and properties Sir Cliges had lost. "For," he said, "if I had a hundred knights such as you, I would be a rich man indeed."

So it was that Sir Cliges returned home, riding on a splendid horse and dressed in fine clothes again. And you may be sure that his wife and their children were most glad to see him, and that they lived a happy life together after that. And, every Christmas for the rest of his life, Sir Cliges held as fine a feast as was seen anywhere in all the land.

As Master William finished, there was a moment of silence, which was broken almost at once when one of the castle servants burst in. "The first of the guests are arriving!" he puffed. "You're all needed to take care of their horses and help them find where they're going to sleep."

The armory emptied in a flash, leaving Master William alone. Smiling quietly to himself, he lifted his tankard and drained the last of the ale. Then he stood up and, with a sigh, went outside into the bustling courtyard to see that the boys performed their duties as they should.

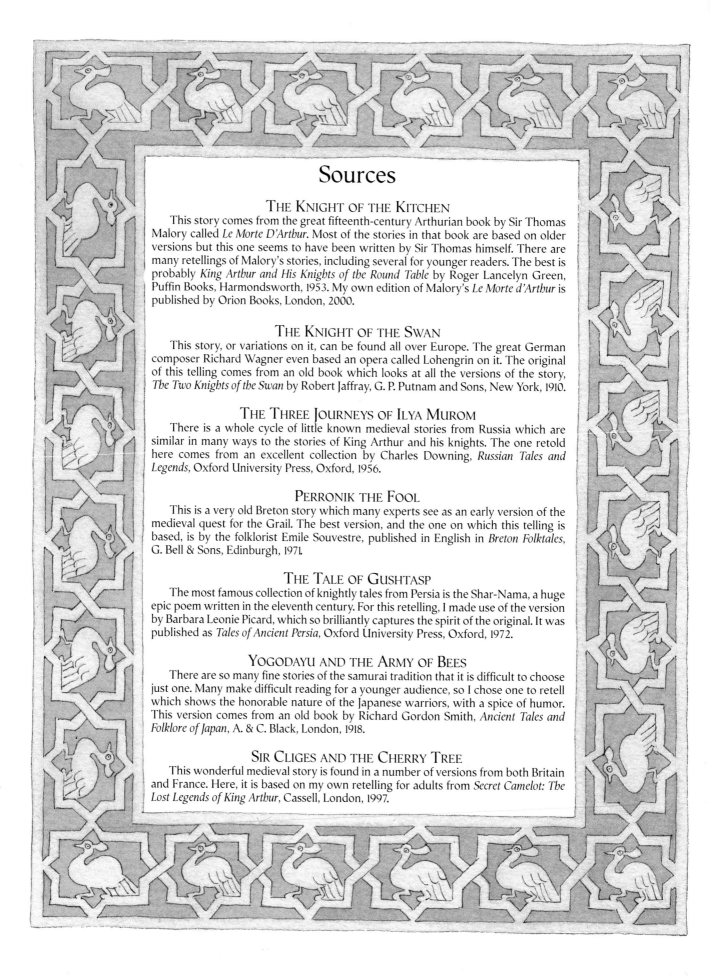

# Sources

### THE KNIGHT OF THE KITCHEN

This story comes from the great fifteenth-century Arthurian book by Sir Thomas Malory called *Le Morte D'Arthur*. Most of the stories in that book are based on older versions but this one seems to have been written by Sir Thomas himself. There are many retellings of Malory's stories, including several for younger readers. The best is probably *King Arthur and His Knights of the Round Table* by Roger Lancelyn Green, Puffin Books, Harmondsworth, 1953. My own edition of Malory's *Le Morte d'Arthur* is published by Orion Books, London, 2000.

### THE KNIGHT OF THE SWAN

This story, or variations on it, can be found all over Europe. The great German composer Richard Wagner even based an opera called Lohengrin on it. The original of this telling comes from an old book which looks at all the versions of the story, *The Two Knights of the Swan* by Robert Jaffray, G. P. Putnam and Sons, New York, 1910.

### THE THREE JOURNEYS OF ILYA MUROM

There is a whole cycle of little known medieval stories from Russia which are similar in many ways to the stories of King Arthur and his knights. The one retold here comes from an excellent collection by Charles Downing, *Russian Tales and Legends*, Oxford University Press, Oxford, 1956.

### PERRONIK THE FOOL

This is a very old Breton story which many experts see as an early version of the medieval quest for the Grail. The best version, and the one on which this telling is based, is by the folklorist Emile Souvestre, published in English in *Breton Folktales*, G. Bell & Sons, Edinburgh, 1971.

### THE TALE OF GUSHTASP

The most famous collection of knightly tales from Persia is the Shar-Nama, a huge epic poem written in the eleventh century. For this retelling, I made use of the version by Barbara Leonie Picard, which so brilliantly captures the spirit of the original. It was published as *Tales of Ancient Persia*, Oxford University Press, Oxford, 1972.

### YOGODAYU AND THE ARMY OF BEES

There are so many fine stories of the samurai tradition that it is difficult to choose just one. Many make difficult reading for a younger audience, so I chose one to retell which shows the honorable nature of the Japanese warriors, with a spice of humor. This version comes from an old book by Richard Gordon Smith, *Ancient Tales and Folklore of Japan*, A. & C. Black, London, 1918.

### SIR CLIGES AND THE CHERRY TREE

This wonderful medieval story is found in a number of versions from both Britain and France. Here, it is based on my own retelling for adults from *Secret Camelot: The Lost Legends of King Arthur*, Cassell, London, 1997.

## Barefoot Books
### *Celebrating Art and Story*

At Barefoot Books, we celebrate art and story that opens
the hearts and minds of children from all walks of life, inspiring
them to read deeper, search further, and explore their own creative gifts.
Taking our inspiration from many different cultures, we focus on themes that
encourage independence of spirit, enthusiasm for learning, and sharing of
the world's diversity. Interactive, playful and beautiful, our products
combine the best of the present with the best of the past to
educate our children as the caretakers of tomorrow.

*www.barefootbooks.com*

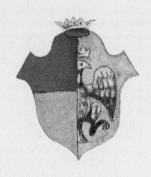